Woozy the Wizard

Broom to Go Zoom

For Josie Camus, my incredible cousin
E. W.

For Mum and Dad
A. M.

First published in 2015
by Faber and Faber Limited
Bloomsbury House
74–77 Great Russell Street
London WC1B 3DA

Designed by Faber and Faber
Printed in China

A CIP record for this book is available from the British Library

978-0571-31115-6

2 4 6 8 10 9 7 5 3 1

A Broom to Go Zoom

by Elli Woollard

Illustrated by Al Murphy

ff

FABER & FABER

In the faraway village

of Snottington Sneeze

Lived a wizard named Woozy

who breezed through the trees.

Up high on his broomstick

he'd flit and he'd fly,

With his Pig at his side

as he sailed through the sky.

Woozy's broom seemed just right –

not too small, not too big,

With a seat for himself

and a perch for his Pig.

But still, it was old,

and was mended in places

With oodles of noodles

and liquorice laces.

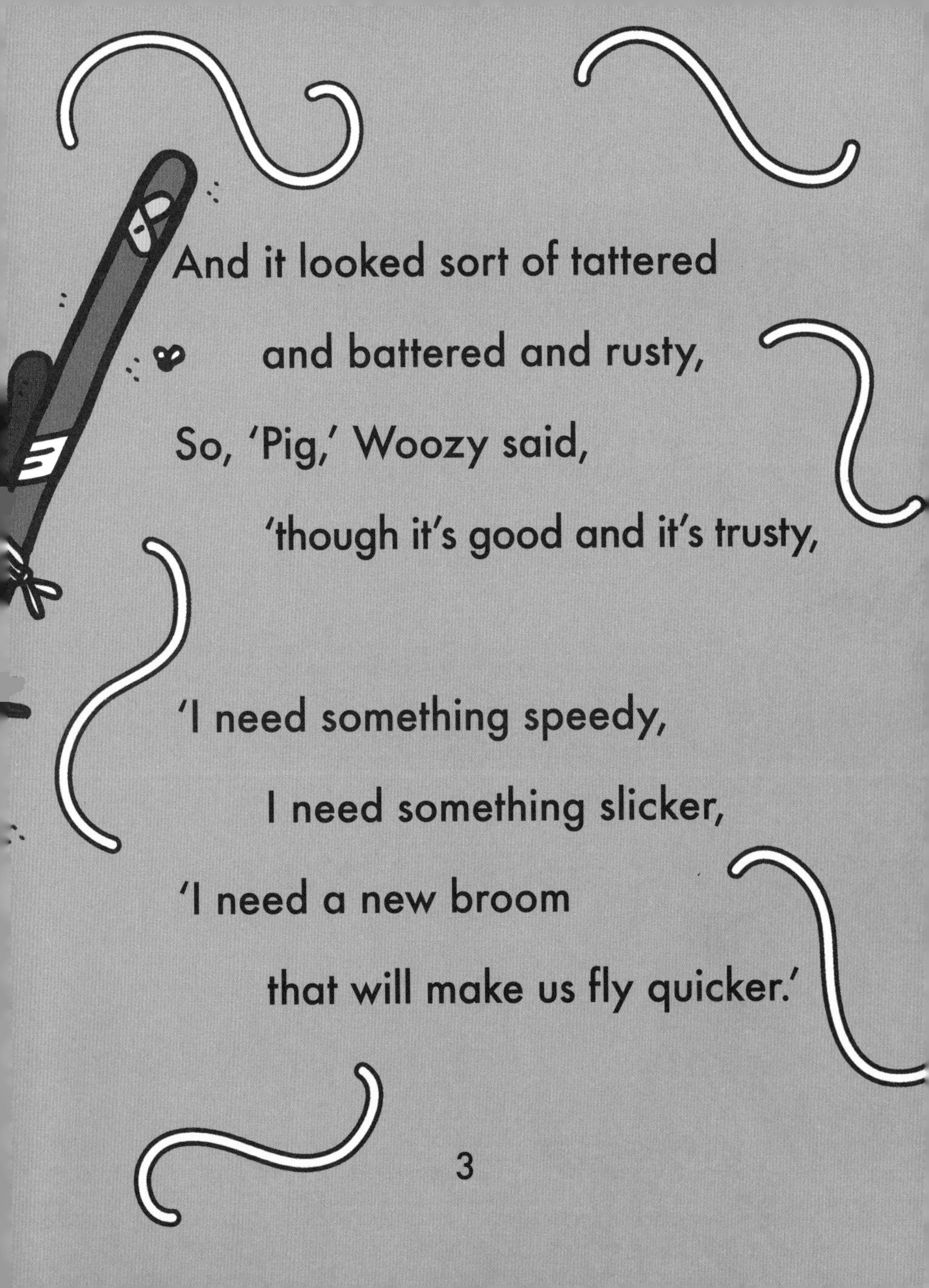

And it looked sort of tattered
and battered and rusty,
So, 'Pig,' Woozy said,
'though it's good and it's trusty,

'I need something speedy,
I need something slicker,
'I need a new broom
that will make us fly quicker.'

Then one sunny day

Woozy screeched to a stop

When he saw a large sign saying,

'Shiny New Shop'.

Underneath, in big letters

and twinkling pink lights

Was an advert that said:

TAKE YOUR LIFE TO NEW HEIGHTS.

IMPROVE WITH A HOOVER;

THEY'RE BETTER THAN BROOMS!

FLY ONE TODAY AND THEN

WATCH HOW IT ZOOMS!

IT'S HERE! POWER VAC 2000!
PAY THIS WAY
TAKE ME HOME TODAY
POWER VAC 2000
POWER VAC 2000
POWER VAC 2000

Woozy shot in through the

shop's open door

Calling, 'Pig, come inside.

I can't wait any more!'

The hoover had gadgets

and nozzles and knobs,

And thingummyjigs

that did all

sorts of jobs.

'It's **brilliant!** It's **zilliant!'**

said Woozy. 'Oh, **WOW!**

'I must have this hoover;

I need it right now.'

Woozy bought it at once and said,

'Pig, how divine!

'A beautiful hoover,

and now it's all mine.'

PAY HERE
POWER VAC
2000

But just as he skipped

through the door of the shop,

He saw Iffy the Elf who yelled,

'Woozy, please **STOP!**

'Hoovers,' said Iffy,

'are really hi-tech.

'Do you know how they work?

I just thought that I'd check.'

FLUMP
LITTER

But Woozy said, 'Sure!'

and he gave a broad grin

As he dumped his old broom

with a 'flump' in the bin.

Then he skipped off back home

and he danced through the gate

Saying, 'Hoovers are fab, Pig.

We'll zoom! I can't wait!'

But as Woozy unpacked it,

he scratched at his head.

'It's not what I thought that

I'd bought,' Woozy said.

For there in the box

was no hoover at all,

Just billions of pieces,

some big and some small.

?
!
POWER
VAC 2000

And Woozy said, 'Pig,

what's all this? Have you seen?

'"Your new flatpack hoover"

– now what does that mean?'

There were gizmos and gadgets

and nozzles and knobs,

And thingummyjigs

that do all sorts of jobs.

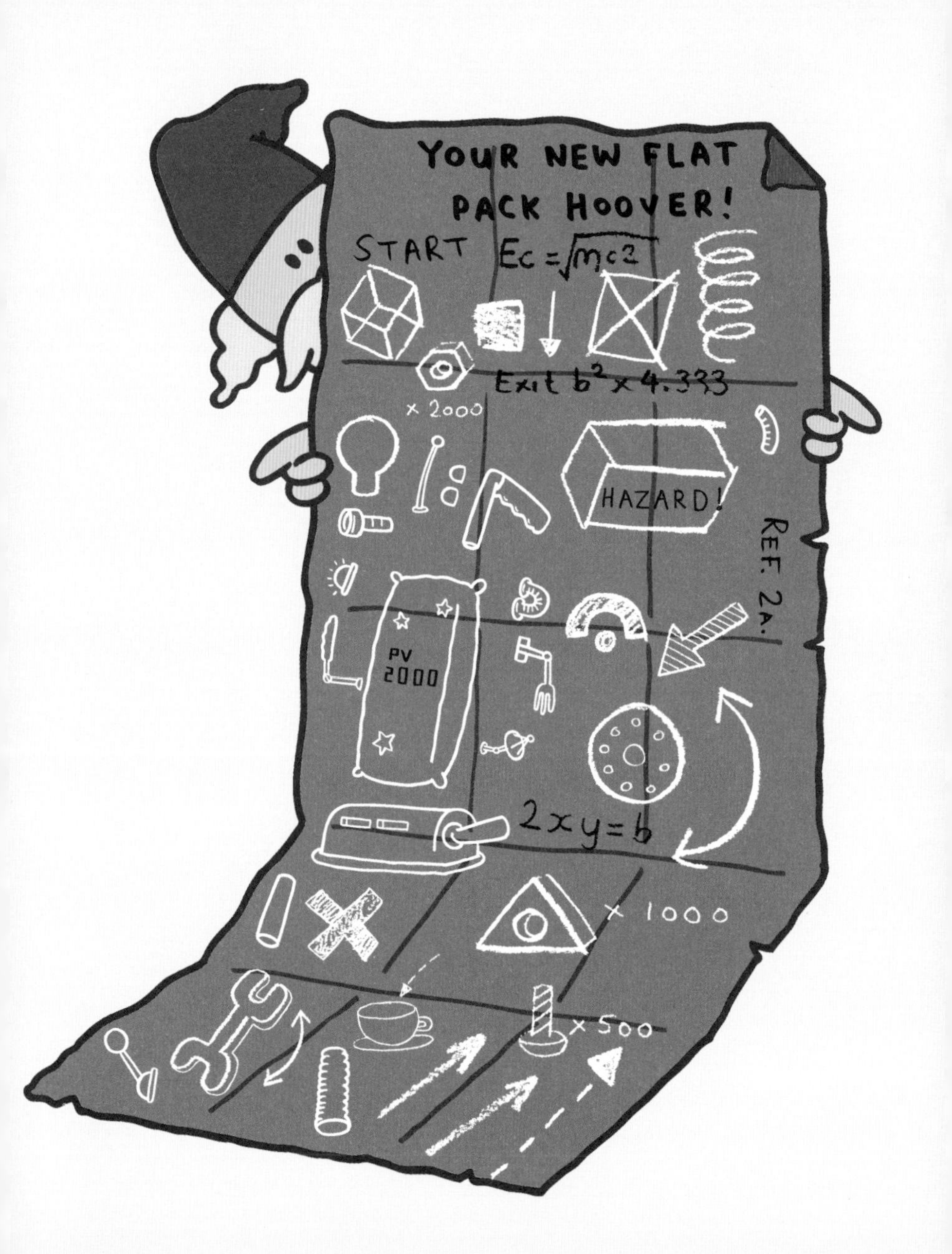
YOUR NEW FLAT PACK HOOVER!
START
Ec = √mc2
Exit b2 x 4.333
x 2000
HAZARD!
REF. 2A.
PV 2000
2xy=b
x 1000
x 500

'But which bits go this way,

and which bits go there?

'And if I switch bits then
which bits should go where?'

'Dear Pig,' Woozy said,
'I will make this thing fly
'If it takes me all night;
I will just have to try.

'Now who can get hoovers
to twirl and to twitch?
'I know who'll help me.
I'll phone up Witch Titch.'

'**Bring bring**,' went the phone
and Witch Titch said, 'Oh, hi!'
And Woozy said, 'Help me!
My hoover won't fly.'

'Woozy!' Titch cackled.

'You **nincompoop** nit.

'Your hoover's not made yet –

it comes as a kit!

'You need globules of glue,

you need screws, you need pliers,

'And hammers and spanners and

wrenches and wires.'

'Now THAT,' Woozy said,

'sounds as peasy as pie.

'I'll soon have this hoover

high up in the sky.'

Then he scratched at his beard and said,

'Pig, there's no glue.

'Oh well, I've got jam –

I suppose that will do.'

But the jam was too gooey
and gummy and gloopy.
It oozed in his shoes and was
smooth and all soupy.

'Oh, Pig!' Woozy cried.
'I've not had any luck!
'I can't move an inch here –
I seem to be **stuck**.'

PLUM
JAM

Woozy said, 'Pig,

I will make this thing fly

'If it takes me all night;

I will just have to try.

'But I must have some help

as I can't do it all.

'I know who'll help me!

I'll call up Witch Tall.'

'Bring bring,' went the phone

and Witch Tall said, 'Oh, hi!'

And Woozy said, 'Help me!

My hoover won't fly.'

'Woozy,' Tall cackled.

'Your hoover won't start?

'Then it's flawed! Then it's faulty!

So take it apart.

'You have to test switches

for problems and glitches,

'As switches with glitches

mean all sorts of hitches.'

'Thanks,' Woozy said,

'I'll test this bit and that,

'And I'll have this thing flying

in two seconds flat.'

So he took off the gadgets and

nozzles and knobs

And the thingummyjigs

that did all sorts of jobs.

But after a while he said,

'Pig, I'm in trouble!

'I'm bathing in bits here,

I'm rattling in rubble!

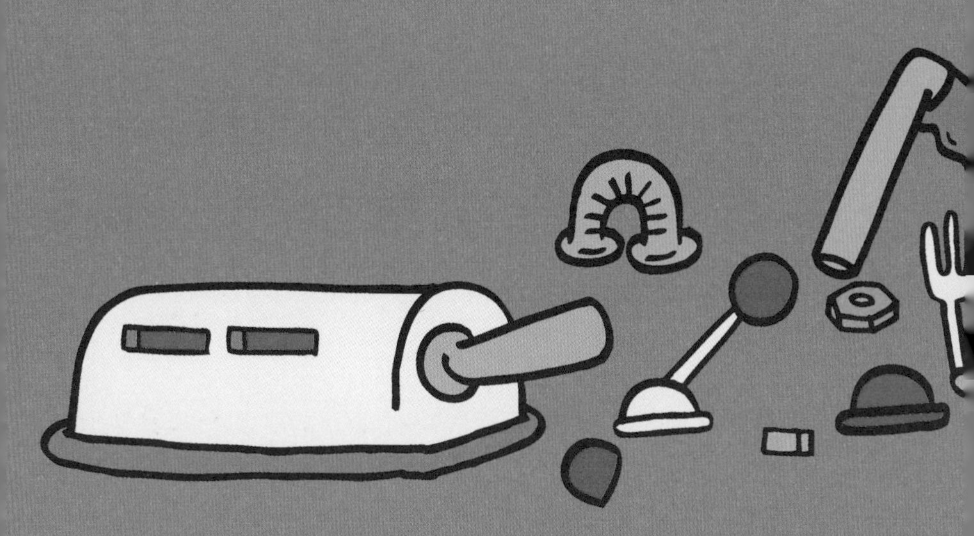

'I've blue screws and new screws.

What could they be for?

'Oh, Pig, it won't work.

I can't take any more!

'Which bits go this way,

and which bits go there?

'And if I switch bits

then which bits should go where?

'Dear Pig,' Woozy said,

'I WILL make this thing fly

'If it takes me all night;

I will just have to try.

'I'll call one more friend.

Who would know? Let me think.

'Maybe Mary the Fairy

of Mouldyton Stink . . .'

Woozy punched in her number

and said on the phone,

'Please come here and help.

I'm no good on my own.'

And so in a twinkling came

Mary the Fairy,

All lumpy and dumpy and

flumpy and hairy.

HOORAYYY!

'Woozy,' said Mary.

'That's tough, I can tell.

'But, my dear, you're a wizard.

Just think of a spell!'

'Thanks!' Woozy said.

'That sounds easy-peasey.

'Just find a good spell

and the rest will be breezy.

'I'll search in my spell book,

I'm sure I can spot it.'

He looked and he looked then he cried,

'Yes, I've got it!

'Abra-ca-donkey

and chocolate éclair!'

And quickly the hoover

rose up in the air . . .

Where it swished and it swooshed

and it spiralled and swooped

And curled in big circles

and lazily looped.

'Pig!' Woozy said,

'Hurry up, climb aboard.'

So they both clambered on then

ZOOM – off they soared.

'Oh, **WOW!**' Woozy shouted.

'We're tickling the trees!

'I don't need a broom

when I've got one of these.'

But just then the hoover

went **sizzle** and **whoosh!**

And wibbled . . .

. . . and wobbled . . .

and crashed in a bush!

'Oh, help!' cried the wizard,
all dirtied with dust.
'My hoover's **kaput**.
It's in bits! It's been bust!

'I know my old broom was all
battered and bashed
'And it wasn't too new, but it
never ONCE crashed!

'Yet I threw it away!

Now I've lost it forever.

'My poor favourite broom.

Pig, I'm not very clever.'

But then round the corner

came Iffy the Elf

Crying, 'Woozy! Oh WHAT

have you done to yourself?

'Thank goodness I've found you.

So *that's* where you are.

'You're the silliest sausage

around here, by far!

'I saw that new hoover

and wasn't impressed,

'And I knew that you'd love your old

broomstick the best.

'So now,' Iffy said,

with a giggle and grin,

'Come and see what I found

when I looked in the bin . . .'

Woozy's old broomstick!

All patched up in places

With oodles of noodles

and liquorice laces.

But still, it was fine.

Not too small, not too big,

With a seat for dear Woozy

and a perch for his Pig.

'What . . .?' Woozy gasped,

'An old broom? Why, it's mine!

'My trusty old broom.

Oh, that's simply divine!

'Thank you, dear Iffy.

Yes, thank you!' he cried,

And he said to his Pig,

'Come on board, take a ride!'

And so, in the village of

Snottington Sneeze

Lives Woozy who soars on his

broom through the trees.

And his Pig gives a squeal

when they zoom and they zip,

As they fly through the sky

and they dive and they dip.

'Hoovers,' says Woozy,

'who needs one of those?

'My broomstick's the best.

Now just watch how it goes!'